RUPERT

and the
TROUBLE
WITH
BIG BEN

CARNIVAL

Rupert is spending a day in London with his pal, Bill Badger. They visit the Tower of London, and then see Westminster Abbey and the Houses of Parliament.

As they are passing Big Ben, a voice whispers in Rupert's ear. "Psst - can you lend me 2p, Rupert?"

Rupert looks round in amazement.
The whisper seemed to have come
from the big clock! "Who said
that?" he gasps.
"It's me - Big Ben," says the clock
in a low voice.

"I need 2p urgently. Can you help me?"

Rupert and Bill fumble in their pockets. "It's all right," shouts Bill. "I've found one."

He holds up the coin for Big Ben to see.
"Thank goodness for that," says the
clock, sounding very relieved. "Now -
come round the side and I'll open the
door for you."

A moment or two later, Rupert and
Bill find themselves standing
inside Big Ben's giant tower!

"Up here," calls a voice from above, and the two pals start climbing the 340 steps to the top!

They are quite out of breath when they arrive in the huge workroom behind the dials.

"Thank you very much for coming," whirrs the clock gratefully. "Could you put the coin on my pendulum, please?"

Bill finds the pendulum and whistles with surprise. It is weighted down with 2p coins and old pennies!

"I need the coins to keep the right time," explains Big Ben. "An extra coin weighs down my pendulum a tiny bit so I tick FASTER. Taking one away does the opposite. They help me to keep the right time all the year round, in summer and winter, whatever the weather."

He gives a sigh. "You can imagine how I felt when I woke up after a little doze and found ONE WAS MISSING!"

Suddenly, a small figure pushing a trolley shuffles out from behind one of the clock's giant cogs. He is wearing tiny overalls - and the trolley is loaded with all kinds of cleaning things plus, on the bottom shelf, a bright shiny 2p coin!

He trundles the trolley across to the pendulum, and with a great effort heaves the shiny 2p onto the pile. Then he sits down, mopping his brow.
"Who are you?" gasps Rupert.

The little figure jumps to his feet. "You shouldn't be in here," he says sharply. "Nobody's allowed in here while we are spring-cleaning."
"Spring-cleaning?" gulps Rupert.

"I suppose you think these coins come clean by themselves," sneers the little man. "Well, they DON'T, I can tell you. It's jolly hard work making them shiny."

"I know you," says Bill
suddenly. "You're one of the
Imps of Spring. I remember
you at Nutwood, painting
daffodils on the Common!"
"Correction," snaps the little
man. "I WAS one of the Imps
of Spring. I'm now one of the
Imps of Spring CLEANING."
He glares at the pals. "And I
can't work with you here so
GO AWAY."

"You're the one who should go away," says Rupert firmly. "Big Ben doesn't need his coins cleaned, and every time you move one, the time goes wrong."

"That does it," cries the Imp furiously. "I'm not staying here to be insulted. I didn't want this job in the first place, and I won't put up with it a second longer."

He peels off his rubber gloves
and slams them on the trolley.
"And don't think they'll send
someone in my place, because
they won't, I'll see to that."

"Well I never," exclaims Rupert
as the Imp storms off, bottles
and jars rattling.

Big Ben chuckles. "Fancy someone being sent to spring-clean my coins! I've never known that to happen before."

"I don't think it's likely to happen again either," grins Bill. He counts the coins on Big Ben's pendulum. "There's one OVER now," he says. "So I'll take my 2p off again."

Rupert frowns. "I hope all this won't mess up your timing too much," he tells Big Ben.

But he needn't worry. As the two pals are leaving, Big Ben starts to chime - at exactly the right moment as usual!

It reminds Rupert of the train
they must catch back to
Nutwood.
"Big Ben's on time but WE'RE
not," he gasps. "If we don't
run, we'll never be home in
time for tea!"

Carnival
An imprint of the Children's Division
of the Collins Publishing Group
8 Grafton Street, London W1X 3LA

First published by Dragon Books 1986
Published in this edition by Carnival 1989

Written by Len Collis
Illustrated by Jon Davis
Copyright © The Nutwood Press 1986
Copyright © title and character of Rupert Bear,
Express Newspapers plc 1986

ISBN 0 00 194457 6

Printed & bound in Great Britain by
BPCC Paulton Books Limited